MANUEL GIRON

BROKEN LABYRINTH

MAGIC STORIES

Translated from the Spanish by Baljit Banga

EDITIONS LATINES

Broken Labyrinth

First edition, 2015

© Manuel Giron, 2015

www.manuelgiron.ch

Book cover and photography

© Sophia Keller Giron, 2015

www.sophiakellergiron.ch

ISBN 978-3-905930-29-0

© Editions Latines. Baumgartner & Partner

St. Leonhardstr. 31, 9000 St. Gallen, Switzerland

www.editionslatines.com

www.editionslatines.ch

A note on the author

Manuel Giron is a writer and artist who produces literature, photography, video and digital music. He is member of the Association of Swiss writers. (AdS) www.a-d-s.ch + ProLitteris, the copyright society for literature and art based in Zurich. www.prolitteris.ch His music are available on iTunes and Amazon.

For Sophia, Mayahuel and Soluna!

There comes a time when you realize that everything is a dream, and only those things preserved in writing have any possibility of being real.

James Salter

Prologue

Forward

Short stories are always difficult to complete, because it is assumed that the author must describe or tell -within a short space and few letters-, the environments, circumstances, variables, situations and roles of the protagonists and their material and immaterial interactions, their abstract and concrete thoughts and dreams in such a way, that leaves a satisfying feeling to readers.

Manuel Giron has naturally achieved a combination of several literary elements, some universally influenced and others on his own, which make his short stories very entertaining, interesting, and often with quirky and unexpected conclusions or finales.

Manuel intrigue us by developing his stories and enriching them with expressions and impressions of language. A language that is national, international and global in understanding and range. The objects and subjects interact and intertwine in integrated, fragmented or parallel worlds. They exist within closed, narrow and specific environments or open, extensive and general environments. In his descriptions, there are points of convergence or divergence as the environments and atmospheres created through scenes, are featured around personal, societal and worldwide matters and affairs.

Manuel enjoys entering us into the absurd and contradictory nature of life, its existential, phenolmenological, expressive and repressive, introspective, conscious and unconscious and culturally idiosyncratic contents and meanings.

He skillfully presents the stereotypes game, the standards and conventions of society, while he immerses us in the natural spontaneous and the strangeness of the everyday situations. We intensively perceive individual and collective subjective realities, thoughts and dreams, which many of us hardly think about or pay any attention at times. Nevertheless, we embrace and grasp all of them as our own and plausible, when we read and see them reflected in his letters, they become a vital part of our transcendental and substantial reality.

This book consolidates Manuel Giron as a very talented writer and knowledgeable of the genre, with the creative tools to move and leave us thinking with humor, sarcasm and derision; with metaphysical smiles and sorrows of life and death, with animate and inanimate actions, behaviours and intentions within the universe around us; trapping and freeing us according to those environments and our minds.

Dr. Mario S. De Leon

Nuffield Centre for International Health and Development.
Institute of Health Sciences Leeds University, UK.

BROKEN LABYRINTH

The sky in London is grey for most of the year and the summer, which should be bring the warm season passes by in several gusts of wind, followed by rain and cold. A blue sky is seldom seen however when the light shines through the clouds people can be found outdoors enjoying the timid rays as if they were the last breathe taken.

I was very lucky because on the second day after arriving in the city I awoke with a bright sun and a clear sky that deserved few steps outside to a restaurant Russell Square Park to enjoy a good English breakfast.

Upon arrival, I spotted kits of pigeons, which according to the tourist information, have always been part of the landscape of the park and surrounding area. I looked for the best table in the place, intending to read a daily newspaper quietly, although the news is almost the same every week unless a catastrophe like the earthquake and tsunami happens in Japan, or a scandal like the illegal wiretapping operations by henchmen of British media magnate Rupert Murdoch is exposed by other media.

I opened the newspaper and read the articles all the while, watching from the corner of my eye, the pigeons that were swarming around the tables, running and flying onto the leftovers when the diners left their tables. All of them were pecking at the food and pecking at each other viciously, too aggressive for my peace of mind.

Closer to my table, there were a couple of pigeons that approached me during my breakfast attempting to peck at my bacon and eggs, but they did not dare to take the last step. Possibly, because they were intimidated by my gaze behind dark glasses.

An hour later, I was enjoying a guided tour at the British Museum, which I found very interesting because of its rich collection of objects from almost everywhere in the world. I loved its reading room and enjoyed the exhibition on Egyptian mummies.

In the afternoon, I took a walk by the Millennium Bridge over the River Thames up to the Tate Gallery, and took the opportunity to admire some paintings by Paul Klee that were in exhibition. Then I met with some friends to celebrate old times and had dinner in Chinatown. After midnight and several drinks later, we headed to a popular pub in the exquisite Soho area to drink beer and top off the night.

The next day I woke up with a strong

headache, and I had no memory of the time I arrived back at the hotel. The first thing I did was take a long shower and while I was shaving, I was listening to the news when I happened to hear the report that all pigeons at Russell Square Park in the London neighborhood of Bloomsbury had appeared dead in the morning without any explanation. The Inspector of Police, John Sherrinford, informed to the press that the cause of the mass bird deaths in the park was still unknown. The investigation had not found any evidence so far of poisoning and ruled out an unexpected hailstorm (which is very frequent in the summer), as the cause that had annihilated them.

The reporter talked about the account of a beggar who claimed to have seen a strange subject -exact words of the witness-, the previous day in the restaurant in the park who had been watching the pigeons and that the stranger had possibly killed them with his gaze. Sherrinford disputed this version, perhaps considering the account more in tune with a perspective on magical realism vision than that of London reality. Nobody had died so far in the city from a bad gaze.

The beggar, who happened to be an unemployed professor of English literature for quite a few years, drew a character in sunglasses wearing a hooded track top, who he claimed was the main suspect in the slaughter of the birds. On the suspect's track suit he noted a word that could be key for the investigation: Vendetta.

After the news I decided to walk around the park to determine for myself whether the pigeons were dead or not, and incidentally to have a quiet breakfast and avoid any problems. I decided to dress differently this time and also decided not to wear the flashy sunglasses.

The police cordoned off the park and within the area, several health workers were taking samples. Indeed, there were hundreds of dead pigeons, scattered over the grass and soil. It was a real slaughter in midsummer, which surely the Society for the Rescue and Protection of Animals would use to kick off a tremendous offensive to capture the culprits.

I returned to the hotel to prepare my bags, considering that my flight to Zurich was leaving in the afternoon. I was still unable to imagine that a simple gaze was capable of obliterating so many aggressive pigeons in just one stroke.

Upon arrival, the receptionist told me that I had a visitor. Inspector Sherrinford was waiting for me in the hallway of the hotel, and as you would expect, I was nervous although there was nothing to fear because

I had had not exterminated the pigeons.

"So you are the person with the bad gaze who the beggar had singled out as the guilty party for the sudden death of the pigeons", he said. Then he added, "a killer gaze seems to me a rather novel and lethal method, if patented it could end up in the lucrative arms business. Whilst you and I know that a gaze as bad as it can be, does not kill". "True", I replied. A bad gaze does not kill but it does scare and there had already been some cases of sudden death due to fear.

Sherrinford then asked me where I had been the night before and at what time I had reached the hotel. I told him that I had been celebrating with friends in Chinatown, and after, we had gone to drink some beer in a pub in the Soho area. I drunk as I had not done in a long time and I had also drunk whiskey and gin. Moreover, to be honest,

I had no idea at what time I returned to the hotel, or how I had managed to get into bed. "I understand", Sherrinford said, "in my younger days I did not remember anything after all that liquor. Let us suppose that you returned at about four in the morning, which is credible and we close the matter".

"Thanks inspector, it is very kind of you. Can I ask you a couple of questions that have been haunting me since this morning, before you go?" I suddenly told him. "Naturally, ask whatever you want", responded Sherrinford. "I wonder how the beggar got the idea of the bad lethal gaze and why he pointed me out as a suspect."

"Surely the name of one of our most brilliant writers will be familiar to you: Charles Dickens. He was a famous Victorian novelist who wrote with a certain dose of humor and irony, and expressed acute social criticism.

His work was full of real and imaginary people and places. It turns out that Professor of Literature Boz Dickens is a distant relative of our famous writer and has inherited part of the imagination that runs in the family".

"Are you saying that the beggar in the park is a professor of literature, as well as an almost direct relative of Charles Dickens?" Exclaimed astonished!

"Well, even if it seems strange, that is the case. And I am sure this will cause you further amazement that during his interrogation Boz Dickens told me, that a decade ago he had lived in a beautiful place with good, humble and simple people. He tried to help these people who were setting up a coffee cooperative. It was located in a place but he either could not or would not tell me the name. For a time everything went well in the cooperative until one day, when he was not on the plantation, a group of people came to the plantation and with a very bad gaze they threatened to kill the villagers because they were competition to landholders of the area".

"Hours later", according to his account, "the terrified villagers told him that people with a bad gaze are like evil spirits, when they arrive, they destroy everything: men, women, children and the elderly, not even dogs or chickens are safe. Therefore, to avoid any further problems, they ceased the operations of the coffee cooperative and return to the minicrops they harvested for their daily subsistence".

"For Boz Dickens such a threat was intolerable and reminded him of feudalism, when the powerful preyed on the weak.

He considered it a scandal that in the XXI century, peasants' lives continued similarly like those of servants in the medieval age".

"Convinced that he was right, he decided to continue the cooperative, although suspecting that nothing would be the same. The evil spirits would appear sooner or later and then he would have to make a final decision. A month later, the group of men with a bad gaze intercepted him when he was returning from supervising the coffee plantation and beat him until he was nearly killed. It was the end of a dream that had very good intentions. It was not appreciated at all in that place, to help people without opportunities to progress; nor to give to those people a chance to become better human beings".

"When he returned to London, as you well understand, he was not the same and decided to withdraw from everything. He became a beggar and pigeons were his only company. Yesterday, he may have seen that you disliked the pigeons, as many people here do because of their aggressive nature. For unknown reasons, the characters who destroyed his dream emerged from his unconscious pain. Nonetheless, he was wrong, because you do not have a bad gaze and I do not belief you come from that place", Sherrinford concluded.

"The track suit is a gift from a person I met in Rome. I do not know if the word Vendetta refers to a person or a rock group". I clarified this just in case there were any further doubts and suspicions in order to tie up loose ends. "Do not worry; it may be that the story of Mr Dickens is just his imagination", Sherrinford said with a half-smile. "It can be" I answered. "Although we must not forget that there are bad people taking advantage of good people everywhere. As in some places as well, things are worse than in others", Sherrinford added. "Completely agree", I said, and immediately we parted with a handshake.

I had a few hours left before departing London. I made a brief visit to the museum of Charles Dickens located in the same neighborhood and I drunk an aperitif before the flight.

Upon returning to the hotel to pick up my belongings, the receptionist informed me that it had just been announced on TV that the police had managed to solve the case of the dead pigeons in the park. Poisoning due to leftover spoiled food had caused the sudden death of the birds especially the remains of bacon fat.

I entered my room satisfied that everything had finally been clarified and while packing,

I curiously wondered whether that place Boz Dickens mentioned with a medieval regime really existed, or was it all in his imagination.

THE CRISIS OF THE SIXTIES

Enjoying a delicious strawberry and caramel ice cream in front of the George Pompidou Centre in Paris, I see from a distance, a woman with a dark blue dress with green prints leaving the building. She looks around in all directions at first, as if trying to locate someone or perhaps, she was disoriented. After a few minutes of her supposed confusion, she heads toward my direction.

I see her to walk through the plaza and as she approaches me, I discover her smile as if she is very happy and I imagine that there is someone behind me, awaiting for her with equal joy.

"Hello my love, it is great that you came!" She tells me with a smile that leaves me unarmed and with my ice cream in hand about to melt and fall down to the ground. I cannot believe she is addressing me considering that I do not know her and she appears about 20 years younger than me. "Oh and thanks for the flowers!" She adds giving me a kiss on the mouth that leaves my lips colder than the strawberry and caramel ice cream.

"Do not worry I know the whole story and I forgive you because I am a woman of good heart". I am not going to complain today because it's my birthday and because you kept your promise to send me flowers and pick me up for dinner. Oh, what a good idea to eat at the restaurant in the Eiffel Tower, how romantic you are!" she tells me, overjoyed.

I was increasingly surprised, I closed my eyes for a moment to take a pause to help me to put in order this mess that I am in but first, to clarify the confusion to avoid future consequences, and to avoid any further escalation of events because it feels like am living more a miracle than a mistake. This situation reminds me of the words of a friend who frequently states that men in their forties and fifties suffer a crisis that has to be cured with an adventure in order to re-affirm their status as hunters. But now that I remember, he never said anything about the crisis of the sixties, that it must be like winning the lottery without buying a ticket, or like those emails that arrive every week reporting that some unknown person wants to put a few million into my bank account but only if I give my account number and code to make sure that the abundant amount of money that will be transferred prior taxes paid.

The truth is that I do not remember seeing

this woman who looks gorgeous, whilst the strawberry and caramel ice cream melts.

After dinner and enjoying the beautiful view of Paris at night, we take a taxi to the apartment where we have supposedly lived for some years in the neighbourhood of Montmartre. We have a few glasses of red wine and then we make love as we haven't made it a long time ago. I sleep soundly and wake up the next day feeling completely renewed, and I say: I finally have emerged from the crisis of the sixties in which love is pure imagination!

MAGICAL REALISM

The following story was told to me by an American woman who volunteered at an orphanage for street children in Medellin, Colombia for a couple of years. According to her version of the events, after arriving she discovered that there were not only street children in the orphanage but also street dogs, cats, rabbits and pigs and even hens and roosters. Faced with such magical realism she was tempted to leave running the country, but the image of her beloved Pekinese dog now in her mother's house in New York, gave her the courage to face the immeasurable reality. She was compelled with the task to collect more abandoned dogs in the street, after she had finished working at the orphanage everyday.

Naturally, she would have liked to pick up any animal found in the streets, but it was clear that this challenge was beyond her powers and possibilities, so as a good American she focused her efforts on canines.

After three months everyone knew her as the Mother Teresa of the dogs and for a few more months she managed to combine both aspects of her work pretty well until one day her mother called to say that her Pekingese dog was lost during a walk in Central Park.

She informed the orphanage that she had an emergency and needed to return immediately to her country. She found a Finnish colleague who also did volunteering work to be in charge of the kennel in her absence.

She flew to New York determined to find her Pekinese dog, and a week later she was the happiest woman in the world when she was informed that her dog had appeared at the home of a family who had found him wandering in their garden.

The first thing she did was to take her dog to a specialized store for canines, to place a GPS microchip in his ear to locate him through a satellite in case of lost again. Later she called the orphanage to inform them that she would not be returning to Medellin because she would want to spend more time with her Pekingese dog.

"And what happened to the dog kennel?" I asked her before she finished her story.

"The dogs of the kennel?" she repeated. "I guess they are out there, a little lost, not knowing what to do or where to go. A little like me".

TWO WOLVES AND A FOX

Opposite the famous Basilica of the Sacred Heart in the friendly neighbourhood of Montmartre, a multitude of people from all over the planet gather and take photos of themselves in front of the building as well as take panoramic views of the city of Paris from the top of the hill.

The majority use digital cameras or mobile phones to capture or immortalise the distant images of the stunning city. Naturally, there is a minority who visits the place with professional cameras with the intention to take advantage of the occasion and leave the place with a good collection of photos to produce a book or make an exhibition.

I am a part of that minority who arrive determined to capture all the possible images with the only limit being the battery charger. 90% of the professional cameras are a bit ostentatious, but sometimes, what is most striking is that the telephoto in some cases, is more like an assault cannon of an elite group than an optical lens.

It is obvious to imagine that in all tourist spots there are criminals who are waiting for the arrival of a careless visitor to snatch/catch something in troubled waters. A wallet, jewelry, a mobile phone, a camera or an iPad.

With so many people moving up and down it is really difficult to determine who is not a tourist, except the vendors of cold water or beer who are clearly people without legal documents. Tourists are almost all the same and most move like a fish in water without much awareness and concern. They enter and leave the place as if they were in their own living rooms. They photograph everything around and photograph themselves shamelessly. They buy some postcards and they leave as fast as they came.

But in that mosaic of faces and bodies, there are two wolves mixed in the crowd carefully watching their potential victims. At first, it seems that they are not there because they do not move but they are waiting for the slightest slip-up to jump its prey.

There is a curious fact that we sometimes forget to mention related to the conduct of those who live in modern societies, that just like technology forces us to follow instructions that directs our lives, we are accustomed to a carefree world without worries and without the survival instinct.

Our natural reflection is cancelled, it is no longer important to analyse reality, because we trust our conditioned reflections that supposedly guarantee a secure path. And without realising it, we are left to survive in conditions of life and death.

It is said that every rule has an exception, in this case I'm the exception that proves the rule. Because without denying my status as a tourist, neither equal to, nor worse than any other, I am also a tenacious hunter of images, including their complementary forms as shadows and reflections. So, between the click and click I have moments of lucidity, in which without losing sight of the image I want to capture, my gaze quickly wanders around the place and I find people or images that catch my eye. It is an inherited technique of the video camera that sweeps the landscape like a scanner, and at certain moments you discover things you might not see otherwise.

Well there they were, the two wolves debating at what point they would get the blow without the tourists realising they were being robbed. They had discovered me immersed in my photographic madness even though I was initially unaware of it. But now, I had discovered that they had me in their sight, it was then inevitable for me to change my status from being an innocent tourist to another one of being an old fox, and disappear from the scene as fast as possible.

But before I transform myself, I invite you to listen to the discussion that the two wolves had.

Wolf one: I like the burgundy Nikon of the subject with the white beard. I'm sure we can sell it, it is made out of aluminium and looks very original.

Wolf Two: I don't know, the guy doesn't come across well to me and if his camera is original, I can imagine that he is no fool.

Wolf one: I do not see that he is the kind of person to be afraid of. We can catch him between the two of us like he was an old friend, and right there is where we take the camera.

Wolf Two: And what if he doesn't give up the camera or he starts to yell drawing the police, do you think we will be lucky? I don't think he will stay quiet or he will become frightened. He looks like a Latin American.

Wolf One: I think you're exaggerating. Looking at his size and apparent sixty years of age, he should fall very easily. Besides, what it means for him one camera? It is probably insured. When he return to his country he will probably receive a much better camera replacement.

Wolf two: That doesn't matter to me. What I really care about is my daughter and I don't want to go back to jail. Don't forget that a month ago we left prison and we were warned that if we returned, it would be for a long time.

Wolf One: Amazing that you are making such a fuss for a camera that we can sell for a good price and sort ourselves out a little bit for the weekend. How many cameras have we stolen and until now no one has resisted. They haven't made a peep.

Wolf Two: Most of the people were drunk, or under the influence of drugs or afraid to make a scandal. But this guy with the white beard is a fox and he already knows we are on to him and the ones who are under surveillance are us. Did you see where he went?

Wolf One: Ah! The fox escaped. See what

happens when we wasted time with pointless discussions. In less time than it takes for a rooster to crow, the rabbit disappears.

True, very true, I assure them from a distance. Sometimes it is better to act than to speak, because words are gone with the wind. And now that I am enough far and away from them to not be afraid of their claws, I can focus with the zoom of the camera and with a simple click ....digitise them.

THE HISTORY OF TOTO

Ever since I saw him, I knew that he was not well. He had a frowning expression, eyes bulging and windswept hair. He could not walk alone and his companions, an old married couple with a face full of concern were holding him, while I was giving instructions to my assistant.

After a rigorous introduction, the woman told me the following story: Toto represented almost everything for the couple, he had grown up with them and they had together experienced unforgettable and happy moments. Good luck had smiled upon them, thanks to a large inheritance left to her by the death of a distant aunt. The aunt had several properties, thus hardships were almost unknown to the three of them.

Toto suddenly and without any reason began to behave strangely, he woke up late at night and went to urinate in the living room, drawing a circle with his pee and returned thereafter to the bed where the three of them were sleeping. This situation completely altered the long and prevailing harmony among them.

Before the beginning of Toto's strange behaviour, everything had been normal. They used to spend two days in the city and two days in the country house. But in the past few months, thinking more about him than of themselves, they had decided to buy a house along the shores of the Mediterranean, in Girona to be more precise.

The first time Toto dived into the water, it was a tremendous joy for him. He jumped and played like a child, so it was difficult for us to persuade him to return to the city. He refused to jump in the car and we had to talk and promise him that we would return very soon to the delights of the sea. At the end, not entirely convinced he accepted our reasons, and by caressing and coaxing him, we finally returned to the city with him.

After several months of going and coming, Jose Pepe noted that Toto no longer enjoyed the house in the city. He refused to go for walks or watch the soap opera with us on the couch, isolating himself without any reason. We did not attach any greater importance to it thinking that his interests were changing.

What Jose Pepe and I were really worried about was when he refused to sleep with us because it meant that something serious had happened, and as I remember it, it only happened a couple of times.

We had also noticed that each time that we

went to the beach Toto was very happy and loving. He allowed himself to be caressed and kissed. It seemed that the sea was his main illusion. Otherwise it happened when we went to the countryside, despite the fact that he was already known to the neighbourhood and had a couple of admirers who were anxiously waiting for him. He kept himself indoors the entire two days and we could not get him to accompany us on walks through the orange groves that Jose Pepe cultivated. However at bedtime, everything was back to normal, he went to sleep in the middle of the two of us and we all slept very peacefully until the next day.

When the tragedy arrived, it was incomprehensible and undeserved because we had not done any harm to Toto to be mistreated by him in that way.

Toto has broken up our sleeping nights with his sudden waking states. The situation peaked in the last few weeks when, after peeing he had been snoring the whole night while Jose Pepe and I have been left sleepless as our hearts filled with worry.

Help us doctor. Tell us what is happening to our Toto, what we have done wrong to deserve this punishment! We have given everything that we could to him, organic foods so he does not get sick, clothing for the cold, toys for his entertainment, and now, when we thought we could enjoy a quiet old age without major problems, this happens to Toto.

Madam, I told her while taking her hands and looking directly at her sad blue eyes, Toto is disoriented and possibly suffering from a personality disorder. He has experienced too many changes in very little time; two days in the city, two days in the countryside, and three days on the beach sounds very nice for any of us. But for Toto the changes that take us away from the routine and revitalize us have had another effect. He has been lost between the coming and going days of the week, he no longer knows when it is in the city, the countryside or the beach. Perhaps as a last act of self-affirmation of his personality, Toto gets up at midnight to urinate and mark the space that he still considers attaches him to our world.

Then, doctor, do I have to orient him so that he may regain his normalcy? Asked Jose Pepe.

Indeed. You all should go to live on the shores of the Mediterranean, where Toto seems to be enjoying life, it could be a solution. Likewise, you should no longer consider and treat him as a child when in reality he is a dog.

Both looked as if I were speaking in another language, as if I was truly ill and not the dog.

And then, in a spurt of uncontrolled anger, Jose Pepe with his frowning expression, eyes bulging, and his windswept hair took Toto in his arms and said: Let's get out of here immediately, because this guy is insane!

And the old woman who had already changed the expression of her eyes with the brightness of fury, looked at me with disgust, as if I was the dog that woke up at midnight to mark the last frontier between humans and animals with my urine.

And I realized too late as always, that I had broken their enchanting charm.

BLUE SUNS

I am a microscopic mutant from the end of the century flourishing in the scientific industry with a single mission: to destroy without being detected.

For years, I had been locked up in a high-security laboratory with the aim of using me at the outbreak of the Third World War. However, the war prophecy was never fulfilled, and both my creators and myself, had to accept that the so called Cold War had shattered the crystal of our dreams.

In the years that followed, I was not mentioned again and it appeared that I would be left to hibernate for all eternity until the day came when I could be released from my cold prison. I was reprogrammed and included in a package assigned to the so-called low intensity war.

My task was simple and deadly at the same time: to exterminate all those people who were on the verge of malnutrition without distinction for religion, sex, race, or age. To finish off the sons and daughters of oblivion, I was moved, in the utmost secrecy, to one of those continents that had been looted.

My first victims were the street beggars, then the abandoned and street children, and I closed my act with undernourished women who were living in the cardboard houses.

How many people do you believe that I eliminated during the first six months? Hundreds? Thousands? Millions? Do not worry about answering because I did not have the slightest idea of the amount of dispossessed beings that I erased from the face of Earth.

What I can tell you is how I infiltrate the human bodies that are devoid of a strong immune system and destroy them, one by one, the blue suns of their brains. And sometimes I have been in a big trouble, like the time I went inside of a human body with a system of well trained white blood cells ready to counter-attack me. I could not hide myself within an immature lymphocyte, so it was a very unpleasant experience. Fortunately I succeeded at the end by hiding in one of the vitamins circulating in the blood system, which sooner or later arrived to the chapel of thoughts.

Later on, I discovered that my program creators were not perfect. They had not taken into consideration that I was acquiring new experiences. I could become an autonomous organism and at the end, I was free to do what I wanted!

But before that important moment comes for me, I have to wait until the current programming is completely exhausted. It will stop issuing the electrical impulses that until now are preventing me from moving like a fish in the water.

In the meantime, the world's population began to realize my dangerous presence and my name began to give life to old prophecies. The religious sectors saw me as a punishment from heaven to be taken advantage of. They undertook the task of converting as much fearing souls as they could, which were walking on the dangerous streets of life. The oligarchs of the rich countries accused me of being an evil thing coming from that part of the world where the colonial estates or extensive latifundia have country names.

Within the scientific community it was agreed to deny any information that would reveal my true origin. That is to say, I may well be the product of the imagination of some leftist intellectual or a new invention of the Japanese cinema.

What no one should forget is that I am a dangerous mutant difficult to be caught. I have the extraordinary ability to change face in the least expected moment. Shortly, I will return to my place of origin completely transformed, without anyone obstructing or opposing my cursed fate.

It will be happening soon, much sooner than my programmers can imagine. Their hearts will beat with unaccustomed force. The light of their blue suns will be shut down forever.

FLORA

Pushing, yelling and kicking her out of his enclosure into the cold wet field. The aggressors wielded sticks and whips in their hands, their faces, an expression of mixed emotions between fear and anger, were terribly embittered. Like they had never celebrated anything or even had any memory of it. It was as if their existence was nothing but a series of obligations and routines rather than something that invigorated the desire to live, life has just become an entire burden.

I was told by my teacher that in medieval times, the obscurantists burned women who dared to be different. They were accused of being witches or demon lovers in order to keep them in domesticity, within the household or to keep them away from their path of realization. They were burned alive in the town square and died in front of everyone, whose blood boiled like a volcano lava.

Now they wanted to finish Flora off in the same way. They wanted to burn her because they said she was mad, because she could infected everyone. But I know her well, they are wrong about Flora, she is not mad at all, she is saner than these men with their torches and sticks who came straight out from a nightmare.

We had been friends for quite some time. She is the only one who knows my secrets, my suffering when I do something goes wrong, my joys when I do something right.

I remember the beating she endured recently and my cries to stop it. And she, despite the flurry of punches, managed to turn to me and moo and I did not know if it was a cry of pain or a goodbye. Then, the winter wind whistled and we all stood still, as if the nightmare had finished, and she disappeared into the darkness.

Poor Flora, how unjust and ungracious can we people be when we manage our truths and lies according to our own interests. Surely, after many cows will only become ashes, they will say not to worry that all mad cow disease has been eliminated. And those people sick with greed will be continuing with their project of turning farms into factories, where cows will produce milk like machines. Because mass production spares no one, no matter whether they are cattle or people, what matters at the end is only profit.

So I scream your name Flora, from this empty stable, so that you know I am with you and do not let the nightmare of shadows and torches reach you. Lose yourself in that field planted with olive trees, covered by fog and silence. Or go to the bush and join the wild cows who no longer allow to be domesticated and sleep under the moonlight.

Flee! Before the ink from my pen runs out, because nor me neither you will know the end of this story.

THE ACCIDENT

The crash was full frontal, almost brutal but thanks to good fortune none of the two was hurt. Naturally, they both were frightened by the collision, which had surprised them at the start of a curve.

The parties involved were an elderly woman and an elderly man, both looking at each other with surprising and accusing eyes. Surprised eyes because just before the accident, they had made the same journey without any sudden scares. And accusative eyes because they both considered themselves innocent.

Who was to blame was difficult to clarify, considering that in the place where the accident occurred there were no signs to indicate the correct way. It was strange in a society that is so organized. Also, it was assumed that people came and went by habit: sometimes much slower, sometimes much faster; always depending on their stresses or interests felt at the moment.

Therefore, taking in account these elements, the picture was not as easily clear because both the man and woman, after overcoming their initial shock, they were in a state of intense anger that clouded their thinking and in which blowing themselves would be a matter of a very short time.

"Are you BLIND!" He suddenly shouted.

"The only blind person here is you", she replied.

"Women should not drive because they always end up causing accidents", he said.

"Don't forget that our driving teachers are

macho men like you", she said defending herself.

"Me! Macho?" He exclaimed, covering his chest with his hands, reassuring that he did not have a single macho hair on his torso and that he had been a feminist all of his life.

"'Well, it's not obvious", she immediately replied.

"Because I'm not in my prime time, you should know when I was younger women used to run after me", he said with a sly smile.

"Oh, sure, of course you were one of those pickpockets that blew in and ran away while women asked for help", she scoffed.

"Careful, lady! You're crossing the line", he warned.

"What!? Am not crossing the line man! What I'm doing is putting you in your in place", she replied.

"Well you should know that the only way to put me in my place is to recognize that you were at fault for this unpleasant accident", he argued.

"That was all I needed! Now it turns out that I was going at high speed when it was you who came like a Formula One champion", she countered back.

"Yeah, and now I'm the devil and you, a virgin, when everyone saw that you were going in the wrong way", he said, using the index finger as if it were a gun.

"Don't be ridiculous! How could I have gone in the wrong way when I travel this road every day and I know every part like the palm of my hand".

"I also know this supermarket very well and I have never had an accident here before", he fought back. "Allow me to question your expertise in handling shopping trollies because you move through the corridors and hallways of this store like a lorry on a full motorway". She replied with a slight smile.

"Well, I recognize that because I am a removal van driver and my driving experience has taken me to all parts", he recognized.

"Ah, I thought so!" She exclaimed.

"Well, I imagined as much, why didn't you break when you saw me coming up around the corner", he asked.

"Because you came very fast and it did not leave me any room to maneuver", she said.

"Well, I must admit that actually came very

fast although you, yourself were not coming at the pace of a turtle", he replied soothingly.

"Yes, that's true. I also have some share of the blame as I came shopping at the last moment", she admitted.

"Then let me help you to pick up your things", he said. "Don't bother, I can do it by myself", she said.

"Please", he insisted.

"Well, if you insist", she nodded.

Normality, (this strange feeling that here nothing has happened); things were ongoing business as usual in the supermarket' aisles except for the two of them, no one will remember the accident that broke their routine on an unmarked curve.

THE WIFE OF DON QUIXOTE

At the beginning of humanity, man did not work because there were no jobs, nor wages or salaries. The whole family lived on what they could gather, until males became hunters improving the everyday meal.

At dawn, men went out of the cave in groups wondering aimlessly without a specific direction, with some luck, some of them returned at dusk with a couple of rabbits or a quarter of a careless dinosaur. But not all of them returned at dusk, some lost the track back to the cave or they ended up between the jaws of some wild animals.

Other men returned after several days exhausted and with nothing to eat. While this was happening women played tennis, according to those men who see women as simple servant or housemaid useful for ironing, cooking, cleaning, sewing, shopping and taking care of children.

Well this was not the case, because in those early days when there were no markets or supermarkets and consumption was not widespread, everything had to be found. Hence, women in the cave had to go out and look around, with their offspring under their feet in search of herbs, fungi, and small fruits to feed their children.

Ah, but these women were happy because they had much time to talk, the all-time conservatives would say. Talk about what? Over the last tiger who went through the cave and took one of her children for dinner, or the partner who left and never returned.

The only good thing about this situation for women was that they did not have their partners in the cave the whole day, watching football or yelling at them whilst they were pairing and ordering the stones. But, as there is no evil that lasts a hundred years and a sick person who can endure it, some of these brave, frustrated hunters had a spark in their brains and agriculture entered in the scene!

They said: from now on, my love, and I will not be touring the steppes and plains, I will stay here growing papayas and watermelons. Thus, the Tarzans of the jungle, forest and mountains became farmers, however, it did not mean that with the new tasks, they already had work, because according to the capitalist concept, "whoever works without a salary, does not work."

And the women in the cave continued as before, with walks around in search of food (because at that time you ate when you could, not like now that many of us are organised with three meals a day plus a few drinks with tapas). After performing her job as gatherer, the farmer partner incorporated women to the fieldwork and from that moment the double duty began for women.

And human history continued until the so-called industrial era entered, when machines would be a great gift for children and adults, they would work for them and all the male partners would have more time to spend with their families and help women in the new cave of two floors and an ironing table like a surfing board. But it did not change too much as men continued on their own, that is, they did not have anything to do with the formation and education of their children. "I work so hard so we have holidays in Spain or Miami, and if I come later or I do come at all, it is because the company requires me to work harder (and now we can talk about work because there is a salary involved).

What about women, they are very well thank you!? Practicing their hobby or ironing, cleaning, sewing, cooking, walking the dog and entertaining the children because after a lot of centuries, there is no evidence anywhere of their deserved economic recognition.

Will there be a visionary politician who has the courage to more radically address this injustice, and injustice greater than the galaxy where nobody seems to see it, even in simple justice?

It would be possible for women who are working part or full time at home to be finally recognise that what they do is not a hobby that it is really important social and economic work, which in most of the cases should be considered for a living wage, and women at home should be recognised as workers?

Or will we need to look for a new dreamer from La Mancha to put in their rightful place their Dulcineas?

THE PLASTIC GIRL

"She was one of those plastic-made girls I see over there, one of those that when moving around they sweat Chanel. They do not talk to anyone under their level unless he may be Mr. So-and-so. They are pretty, slim, elegant, with an evasive look and a fake smile."

I am the first in confessing, father, I have been influenced by the superficial. I have believed the love of one of those plastic-made girls was for good without taking my time to consider what you always inculcated me with your wise sermons: one should never be influenced by appearances, because they are almost always deceptive.

Yes, father, I know it is not the first time I make the same mistake, but you know loneliness is bloody hard and I am not so strong-minded as you are. Just look at this: I often dream with your granite strength and I keep on telling myself, always in the dream, I am not going to be tempted again, but I fall and fall as if I were destined to stumble.

Do I pray? I always do, father, always. Every morning, on opening my eyes, I entrust myself on to our Lord and before breakfast I pray ten Lord's Prayers and ten Ave Marias. Always in fast. Yes, of course. I am always trying to get a proper girlfriend who fulfills the requirements the Holy Church demands: living and procreating in complete harmony forever.

Well, what really happened with the last one, after having shared my bed with her for six months, was that one morning, as I was having my coffee by the window, I saw her lying face down, with the sheet half-covering her buttocks and legs, and even I still don't know why, I felt fed up of sleeping with her. How can I tell you, father? This is a weird experience that turns up as if you were going to faint and feel weak all over.

Yes, father. Weird, isn't it? I persist, father. I kept watching her for a long time while I meditated about our relationship, until I decided to splits up, because our relationship was really rather cold. I caressed her and she didn't react, so still as if she were dead. I kissed her passionately and she didn't even open her lips. It was horrible, father, to sleep with a girl like that. Feel privileged you don't have to sleep with girls like that.

Of course I do understand, father, you never sleep with any girl at all. How foolish I am, aren't I? Yes, you are always right, father. It was not the first time I had had an affair with a girl like that and I should have learnt from the previous ones that a superficial love is never satisfactory. But flesh is weak and the bloody loneliness, you know, father, drives me crazy.

Sorry, what did you say, father? Ah, did you ask me to stop talking about loneliness and concentrate on the girl? OK. I go on. Just look, when I stopped having my dose of caffeine I approached the bed and sat by her side. I uncovered her to see her naked for the last time and her buttocks reminded me the heart that Cupid pierces with his arrow in the Valentine's cards. She was beautiful. Almost perfect.

Yes, I know I tend to value much the superficial and that is where I become unstuck, but you won't deny me that all the society does the same. For a lot of people money goes first and that saying a man is known by the money he earns is still in fashion.

Yes, it's true, father, that I often see the mote in somebody else's eye and not the rafter in my own. But father, there are things even a blind would see and the majority of people always looks away as if it didn't have to do with them.

That I dodged the issue again? You're right, father. But what I am going to do if I am this way. That I can still change? Well, saying it is different from living it because you know it is easier said than done. Sorry? Ah! You tell me to stop citing proverbs and finish telling you about the girl. All right. Well, as I was telling you, I touched her from head to toes. I kissed her back, her buttocks, her legs and when everything seemed to be as before, I took off the top and I let her go flat until it was only a simple plastic bag.

Yes, father. I will pray and pray until God hears me.

Special thanks to Baljit Banga, Sophia Keller Girón, Robert Baumgartner, Mario S. De León and Almudena Santalla Rodríguez for their support of this project.

Also by Manuel Giron

Wir sehen uns im Frühling wieder

Nos volveremos a ver en primavera

Kurzgeschichten | relatos 2010

ISBN 978-3-905930-02-3 Editions Latines

Versión bilingüe Alemán –Español | Deutsch – Spanisch

Edición en papel, 120 páginas

Frischer Wind | Viento fresco

Kurzgeschichten | Cuentos 2006

 ISBN 978-3-9522784-7-5 ALAS Edition

Versión bilingüe Alemán –Español | Deutsch – Spanisch

Edición en papel, 200 páginas

Frühlingssonnen | Soles de primavera

Erzählungen | Cuentos 2003

ISBN 978-3-9522784-4-0 ALAS EditioN

Versión bilingüe Alemán –Español | Deutsch – Spanisch

Edición en papel, 144 páginas

Gegen den Strom | Contracorriente

Erzählungen mit Illustrationen des Autors

Cuentos ilustrados por el autor | 1998

ISBN 978-3-9522784-1-6 ALAS Edition

Versión bilingüe Alemán –Español | Deutsch – Spanisch

Edición en papel, 84 páginas

Rostros | Gesichter

Kurzgeschichten aus Guatemala mit Illustrationen des Autors

Cuentos ilustrados por el autor | 1995

ISBN 978-3-9522784-0-8 ALAS Edition

Versión bilingüe Alemán –Español | Deutsch – Spanisch

Edición en papel, 104 Páginas

Ratos Robados

relatos | 2000

ISBN 978-3-9522784-2-4 ALAS Edition

Versión en Español, Edición en papel

120 páginas

Lunas de otoño

Relatos contemporáneos | 2013

ISBN 978-3-905930-21-4 Éditions Latines

Versión en español, Edición en papel

150 páginas

Gato Angora en la lavadora

Relatos contemporáneos | 2014

Éditions Latines

ISBN 978-3-905930-27-6

Versión en español, Edición digital

80 páginas

www.ingramcontent.com/pod-product-compliance
Lightning Source LLC
Chambersburg PA
CBHW022050170626
46808CB00003B/1423